Miles

T3-BVI-172

Mon.	Input	Mic			
	TRUMPET (RF)	* D.I.	17		RACK 2-3
	SPARE (RF)	B.S.S. D.I	18		RACK 4-5
	SPARE (RF)	* D.I.	19		RACK 6
	SAX	* D.I.	20		FLOOR 1
	FLUTE	* D.I.	21		FLOOR 2
	OBX	* D.I.	22		O.H. LEFT
	DX-?	* D.I.	23		O.H. RIGHT
	KEY (LEFT)	* D.I.	24		BELL TREE
	KEY (RIGHT)	* D.I.	25		PERC. (LE
	BASS (PRE)	* D.I.	26		PERC. (RIG
	BASS (F/X)	MD-421	27		M.C./SPA
	BASS (MIC)	PL-20	28		
	LEAD (LEFT)	PL-20	29		
	LEAD (RIGHT)	* M-88	30		
	KICK	S*-57	31		
	SNARE (TOP)	SM-57	32		
	SNARE (BOT.)				

All others will be provided by

Bass

Percussion

Kick
Saare (Top)
Saare (Bottom)
Hi-Hat
Rack 1
Rack 2-3
Rack 4-5
Rack 6
Floor 1
Floor 2
Overhead Left
Overhead Right

Bell
Tree

ITOR
ESK
ST BE
AGE
IGHT

Keys

OBX
&
DX-7

Lead L

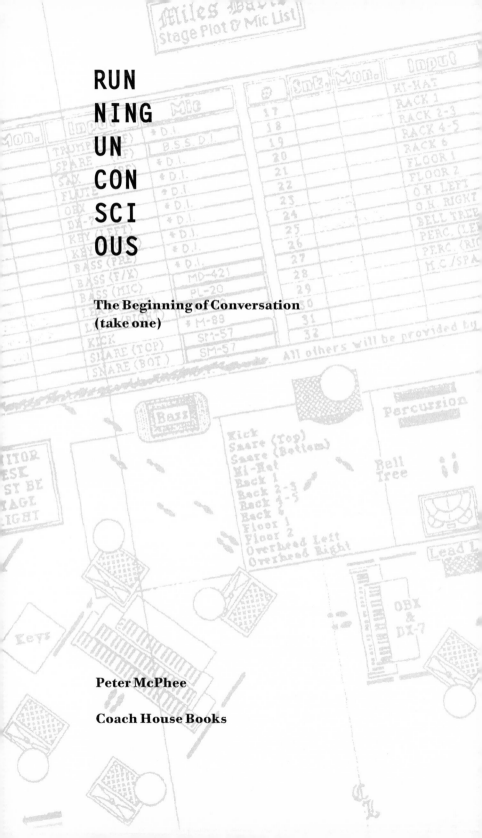

RUN NING UN CON SCI OUS

**The Beginning of Conversation
(take one)**

Peter McPhee

Coach House Books

First Edition

FULL TONAL RANGE ||||| ЅТΞꓴΞꓴ ||||| COACH HOUSE Y2OK

CANADIAN CATALOGUING IN PUBLICATION DATA

McPhee, Peter, 1964 -
Running unconscious: the beginning of conversation (take one)

Poems.
ISBN 1 55245 078 3

1. Title.

PS8575.P445R86 1999   c811'54.   c99-933006-3
PR9199.3.M33687R84 1999

for John & Nancy McPhee

You play saxophone, right?
Well, the music is on the horn.
Between the two of you, you should be able to find it.

Thelonious Monk,
explaining his charts
to Coleman Hawkins and John Coltrane

LISTEN
WHEN
THE
HEART
BEAT

an
introduction
by Seán Virgo
August 1999

listen
　　when the heartbeat, the ocean-cleaving turbine in the
foetus's ears, is depthcharged and drowned by
　　　　the boombox-pulsing transam / cherokee / z28
beside you, in moronic dalliance with the red light
　　when the woman on the streetcar, the only person
aboard who thinks and speaks in actual sentences, went to
school in barbados
　　　　and the bass line of the porno movie in the apart-
ment downstairs where the people live on fried bacon
　　when the man who swabs the subway steps at queens
park has a doctorate in sanskrit poetry from the u of
bucharest
　　　　and the wank-wank gang-bang bully-boy rappers
on the taxicab radio, passing the clinic, the safe-house, the
Munch-kin outpatients
　　in this kakistocracy, soft minds with hard sells and
noses, who would fold at the hint of invasion, who would
scurry to be police informers, who can shrug and say 'sorry,
we were wrong' and not have to mean it but walk away, vicars
of BRAY
　　　　and the golden-oldies, ten-without-talking,
sugar shack, lollipop, honeycomb, oh sugar sugar, candy for
impotent strangers
　　out in the concrete canyons, where blind moondog may
be wailing still for his demon lover, where the tambourine
girl may still be preaching the jingle-jangle, the chinkle-
chankle, the dawn, where the still sad music must still be
afloat, but
FIAT CLAMOR
　　no one can hear them ...
I came to the valley of tin ears
and a voice from the canyon walls cried out
shall these ears prick up and hear? Again? Ever again?

and halfway to the fifth floor, between the boardroom
and the thousand violins, we heard the grunt of the chains
in the blind shaft: earbone disconnected from the head-
bone, headbone disconnected from the heartburn ...
          stockhausen gesturing through the cage:
     make music out of it ...
          in the warren where he listened to air-conditioners
hum: a threnody for dishwasher, bubblejet printer, garbage
truck backing up beep by the fire-escape, jackhammer down
by the park, big jet coming in, the licensed music of the
motorized spheres on the gardiner
          through it all the sirens sound almost human

you can flee to walden like my kind
                    you can saddle the energy like mcphee
     smiling, inventing, lamenting, remembering – singing
despite the tin ears
          making it human
          what is he up against?

the métis mad prophet saw it, he called it a giant, 'its name
is Goliath.'

five little stones from the kerith brook: laughter, wonder,
mockery, memory, song:
          each one a killer, each a saviour

peter mcphee is a dancer, the giant across the stream doesn't
get it, he can't hear the music, the rules have been changed,
a slingshot for god's sake, does he think this is recess? the
damn kid is laughing ...

and somehow this brings us home again *

the night plays bottleneck and spoon
 four thousand years too intelligent to fall in love
 Sometimes / I stand in line / all day / letting others
ahead of me
the clear run of peak to stream / the trailing voice of an old
story-teller's love song
 Sir / it is cold / I am cold sir
 sound erodes / waterfall feather / a measure of time
so small / it has to seem like forever / for anyone to remember
 yes I love you / but sometimes / I wish you would /
please stop talking
 a soft shock of colour
 And someone downstairs reading / the ride of
Paul Revere
solitude hanging from their shirt sleeves / as if they stopped
playing for a moment / a million years ago
 there are bigger tragedies / get over it
 the roof caves in between us
it's not what he had in mind / he's against the war generally /
but it happened so quickly / and now / there is mud
 the splinter of ballots burning
 And sunset's greygreen marble / closes black the
inside of a body bag
 the rain stops / for the last time maybe
 with any luck I'll still be breathing
 oblivious to everything / but the pauses in his song

* *after randall jarrell's collage, the best, the only*
  critique of walt whitman

and a
wave
means
we are
not
drowning

There have been centuries before
                    I suppose

we're here now
washed light through a cool basin sky
a colour that will not tell the secrets of landscape
had this place been discovered
                              it would be morning
because we're awake
                    we are less simple

sleep drains wine from cornea glass
the way the earth forms our backs
why rise
          unless it's not all *up* from here
plateau stretching to mist
and likely something   looming

a thought:

these arms and legs beg movement
and turn your head   (tentative
     we might not work this way)
see for the first time beside you
my head turned also
where I've been watching for a long time
your flow
          dark metallic pool to blue skin

of all the things you don't know
                         am I solid
the names to discover
               rock perhaps   *slug*   or *tree*
the questions we are unsure how to phrase
how we first realize the *more than instinct*
control of spinning   quiet
                         desire

touch
much less touch our own fingertips
magnets of equal pole send
electrons circle forearms
intersect the spine
are drawn to the nerve end
of opposing fingers
and burn there

or what it means to listen
when unaware our breath
the long calm exhale in the air
a body of water close by
floating wind across the crag and scar
of all those centuries before

the sound of filling hollow

you'd think there'd be something to say
a progression on the evolution of stone
a misunderstanding of melody
we will one day perceive
as an accident of birth

we lie here missing
not quite you and not quite a rock
unsure and dangling
our only hope for complete
resting on a gesture not unlike
the gentle raising of a hand
a first shy offering
                    hi
and can't fail in this
yet likely hear nothing in return
until we add
            may I help you?
gain perhaps   a turning of the head.

So let's say time passes
we learn our arms and legs
and walk awhile
and find   close by   fresh water
and kneel
            submerge our heads
                        just looking

and let's say we also stand along the shore
to watch ourselves kneel
heads submerged
not knowing what we see there
denying how ludicrous it seems
after all   it's us
and we'd prefer to think this
the natural order of things

it remains this way for a long time:

us on the shore
our heads under water
eyes open until eventually
someone blinks
   (accepts this also as natural)
a distortion of light rising to surface
cresting to ripple
a measure of distance
something to stare off into

the beginning of conversation

                    we are talking to ourselves

and you are not supposed to feel this way
no more shyness
four thousand years too intelligent to fall in love
the small part to be included
and all the great things we've come to expect from you

it's late morning on the fire escape
when I tell you of Lake Minnewaka

my body's imprint on rock
the glacial blue reflecting
the Cascades' rise from the far shore
and *have I ever been more at peace?*
my heat-blurred vision
a tern circling

circling an effortless coast and glide
as I watch and wonder
do birds simply fly for the joy of it
circling and easy
changing path as if to say
I am leaving you forever
the water remains   as cold   as sweet
dissolving into mountains
I can't be sure it was ever there

or is it afternoon
driving the colour of wind in your hair
we pass that first breath of fresh water
its blond reflection dancing
and see something floating there   and gone
the way the sun is sometimes

we could leave without a trace
	a moment to lose
or we could check the mirror for surface
turn our heads
could've been a body
a sea monster
a tree so old on the edge of a lake
before there is such a thing as lakes
with initials carved
that is hit by lightning
that is bleached in the sun

the question is not whether this time
there are gloves in the glove compartment
but do we need to search there

knowing the way you unfold time
I follow the ancient road-maps
to the feeling I have sometimes
your fingers through my hair
as you   miles from here   *touch*
candles burn suspension
an invisible wax drip dew
beads your skin   warms you

I feel the heat

ACCI
DENT
AL
SOM
ER
SAULTS

Agence spat...
canadienne

Canadian Space
Agency

4e étage
Place Air Canada   ...que Ouest
500, boulevard ...
Montréal (Québec
H2Z 1Z7

4th Floor
Air Canada Building
500 René-Lévesque Boulevard West
Montréal, Québec
H2Z 1Z7

ch 19, 1992

923E
r. Peter McPhee
73 Palmerston Blvd #3
Toronto, Ontario
M6G 2N9

Dear Mr. McPhee,

This is to acknowledge receipt of your application
Astronaut.

The Agency has had the challenging
relatively small number of candidates from among
interesting applications.

Your submission was carefully considered, but
unable to offer you employment.   Shou
become available within six months, we will be
with you again.

Yours sincerely,

*what is
the most important thing we can think of
at this extraordinary moment*

Do Not Fold   Spindle   or Mutilate

Between handle bars
and curb
        a lack of friction
the locked-break chipped-tooth surprise
as tongue stumbles and
why the mountain bike wasn't your idea
it doesn't work that way —
thinking of things to sell

the toboggan leaves the cliff
you leave the toboggan
those old cartoon tumbles
ava-launch and airborne
the tree comes at you

a difficult cycle to capture

Saturday morning's sit 'n' spin
Spirograph battles Hurricane Hank
the animated feature
the space between line drawing
                              and colour blur
filled by computer now

the optical reader in high school
hours with pencil   computer cards
keep edges clean in a shoe box
wave a hand over
say magic words
                    Job End Run
mail to the phone company
and one week later
you're told whether you have aptitude

e) all of the above

I have a joke for you:

   artificial intelligence

   the Robot and Dr Smith
   reach a binary understanding

   shut up

                              start talking

Healthy now
dressing fluid
drinking plenty of warm liquid

no longer calling in my sleep –
things like *Patch Cords* or
Don't shoot   I've got aptitude

no longer a dim light office prowler
on the copy addict help-line
toll-free Xerox exorcist talking down

more the old black and white's grey blue dance
through to the street side of your bedroom window
and even with the sound off
two am commercials sell in stage whisper:

ARE YOU SUFFERING
FROM DEPRESSION

I am water draining clockwise in a northern hemisphere
and someone hands me a plunger
or a matchbook:

Be an achiever
order our free career booklet
computer hotel management
vcr firearms repair

the correspondence school of art

Do Not Mail Matches
Do Not Pass Go

the thing is
I'm not sure how to thank you

Let me introduce you
to the guy in the basement
inventing earthquakes
his hands are tremors
you can feel through the baseboards
pushing us to accidental somersaults
we land
          running unconscious

come to with me
and I'll show you my tattoo
everything I've learned
in six words or less
written in small print
on my instep

see the way it curves?

a girl in summer print
followed it with her finger
and disappeared

she left directions to her tree house
it's not far   but well hidden:
cross a brook a highway an old dirt-road
turn left and   if you promise not to tell
I'll write them in a note to you
with secret code

be sure to swallow it

Lost in Translation

Hanging out under lazy fly balls
ice-cream vendors are forever
a pomegranate snow over where
the outfield fence has come down
someone along the third row
is making rules in lipstick
wiping them away
and anymore
there's no sure thing as a home run

losing in the sun and everything
did you see that wave?
it was brilliant
what's that green oceans are
transparent before the cap
confusion and froth
as dogs rush past   dissolve
and leave those perfect paw prints

how slow free fall feels from down here
while physics concentrates in books
crumbling and sensitive to light
why waste water resolving facts
you could drink a whole pitcher
open throat and dribbling
ice-cubes rolling

the hours oil a glove for this moment
one could attend opera
slightly embarrassed to be seen in such company
wishing they'd lose the surtitles:
those free tickets to *Romeo et Juliet*
and all I remember is
WHAT'S THAT LIGHT OVER THERE IN THE WINDOW
in subway platform letters

you're pretty sure I was conscious
though feeling like that time in Montreal
Neil and I drink the afternoon
trade bad haircuts
and the Dali exhibit guard
who three times warns me to stand back
to stop reflecting elephants with swans
while Neil adjusts the mirror
to the *Skull*'s distortion
and nothing is clear to the patio the margaritas
and the Modern Jazz Quartet
where I sleep soundly in the back row
waking briefly to applause.

The sound
how your hand fits to the pocket broken in
and even if we never attend a meeting to prepare
the question of its waiting to be caught is posed.
Are we so simple as to care
if the last puzzle piece is missing
or only tired of fables?
Casey At The Bat
Pelléas et Mélisande (as Patrick tells it)

Golaud a prince is lost in the woods
where he finds Mélisande who is crying:

  Why are you crying he asks
     Don't touch me. Don't touch me.
     (she says everything twice)
    I won't touch you. I'm a prince. Has someone hurt you?
     Yes. Yes. Everyone.
  Where are you from?

I escape   flee   run away.
… from where do you escape?
I'm lost   lost   I don't belong here.
…where do you belong?
Far far away.   But why are you here? Prince.
I don't know.

he doesn't know
the prince doesn't know why he's there
and then asks Mélisande to go with him

No thanks.   I'll stay here.
You can't stay here alone.   Give me your hand.
Don't touch me.
I won't touch you.   Come with me.
Where are you going?
I don't know.   I'm lost too.

and they leave
not even the home half of the seventh
a slow leak in the blimp only just discovered
umpires gather suspects in the drawing room
what goes up goes on vacation
and those big   stupid   blind dogs
materialize   way off   racing the horizon

and I am still here
rethinking where the lotion's applied
what to do with an ice-pick   a glacier   a piña colada
and you have left your body in front of that line-drive again
go get it
lay it where nothing ends the landing of a baseball
and we'll forget how the waves are drifting
hope no one will ever cut the grass

Planning a Haircut

feeling the way your arms rise after heavy lifting
and knowing your legs go the same way
you let them

and lying here
you can see the mountains' circle
a year ago Thursday
watching snow caps melt
through shades of rose and blue forest green

the holes in the sky mountains fall through

stars cool and precipitate
land weight against weight
contour   channel
glacial spring come ocean
continents rise
life forms
and the pressure turns inward
circumference pushing to core
every wish we make
compressed to a single flame

tomorrow you will climb against this current
and weeks later tell John on his rooftop
how on reaching a canyon
below the peak of Mount Rundle
just above the tree line
you scramble up loose shale and turn
to see the trail erode three thousand feet
feel your body follow
and afraid even to climb down
freeze against the rock face
vertigo

and John will say
You mean
you have to climb down?

Thoung joins you hillside
Vietnamese through Montreal and now Vancouver
of all her language
she writes poetry in English
like speaking through a third person
and poetry is of oneself

stepping outside himself
he winds up in the final scene of *White Heat*
Cagney on the summit of some burning tower
raging to flame   *Look Ma   top o' the world*

(I've been here before
my fears remain   )

in *Strawberry Blonde*
he's an Irish mail-order dentist
who takes the fall and gets the girl
That's the kind of hairpin I am

(you can't fall off a mountain)

and somehow this brings us home again
Toronto   today
where spring has come for the first time
almost a natural occurrence

I am light easy refraction
I'll maybe do something to save the world
pay more attention to personal appearance
to how things look through
the rose-shaded green of your eyes

and when you ask I'll say
Everyone's in Florida today
and I can't
            for the life of me
imagine why

First Impression of a Double Rainbow

You saw a double rainbow for the first time
and I wonder why reflection   a constant
is rarely in view
the science opposing spectra
reaches no conclusion

sometime before then
careless and strong
we find ourselves climbing
the gap between summit and space
cutting our packs loose
fear drops a thousand spinning feet

after descent:
clear afternoon
the moon rests
at the peak of Mount Temple
sound erodes
waterfall   feather
a measure of time so small
it has to seem like forever
for anyone to remember

sometimes
a child wishing a balloon
I know the moon to filter through
a cool cloth against fever
I am here now
        close your eyes

Vernal Equinox

I found Phelix on Queen Street
trying to unload April at four a.m.
He wasn't getting any takers

Phelix was the type of guy whose prospects
wake up in the morning   shiver
and think better of daylight

writing letters in a windowless room
Sir
   It is much too cold
   I am much too cold sir
   Please turn on the heat
he only went out to warm himself
a bar where he was the only regular
and no one asked questions
he'd sit on his stool and look forward to April

April hadn't been around much lately
rumours gusted from other tables
winter's tattoos already on May
Phelix couldn't happen that way
saw himself as the last-ditch effort
he was long past writing letters
Sir
   It is cold
   I am cold sir

he scooped April with his shoulder bag
discarding his notebook to make room
all the letters he'd written
dissolving in the mad March slush
he ran up an alley
left winter forming ice-bridges
on the far side of a month-long gap

for the first time since the sun went down
Phelix was smiling
a warrant was issued for his arrest
and I was trying to get word to him

so there he was
trying to unload hot property
'cause he'd been so damn cold
he looked at me   melting ice-cube eyes
and grinned a kid   a snowball in July

meanwhile north and east joined forces
winding through the restaurant district
Phelix heard them coming
slipped something in my pocket
April is on the way he said
and melted into the sidewalk

walking home I read the letter he gave me
ink running
Sir
   It is cold
   I am cold sir
I heard his sound to save spring
fall the five stories of inside-room madness
and settle into a silence that
someone will soon call summer

Leaning against a lamppost
on the corner of King and Diversity

flipping a quarter
deciding which call to make
when out from a half star lounge
slips the lost letter of a '63 love affair

she thinks about crossing
instead   meets my eye
asks: *do I know what life's about?*
Life's about four feet tall
balding
and a block up the street
turning left in a rusted volkswagen

she winks a wide revelation and
leaving an exhaust fume
runs off   screaming
follow that car

chasing after elusive movement

I was almost born in the back seat of a moving object
we made it in time to forgo any legends
and I am named
not after some cabby or coincident cop
but after the solid earth and my grandfathers

my birth was in the tradition of this civilization
no one looked in my eyes
calling *Lake of Moons* or
Blue Sea on a Misty Day
and that only bothers me
meeting the eyes that pass here
naming their children after television
and following that short balding man to the end of the day.

I have a friend named Sabre
quiet   sharp
a laughing blade through sunlight
she dazzles   inspires my direction
through so many choices
to a decision that leans toward
something dangerous

I want to step in the street
flipping quarters
risk everything
but the possibility
of at least one more call

to hear someone say
Hey
        what are you trying to do?
Get yourself killed?

no

and if I'm blind sided
by something empty and personal
as *not any more*
I want the bus to hit me mid-dream
my eyes wide
so no amount of currency will close them
a phone booth somewhere
ringing and ringing
my funeral in the back of a cab
at ninety miles per hour
and my body hurled to a ditch
by the side of the road

with any luck
I'll still be breathing

Raspberry Ripple

This wild raspberry kind of oodles over and
explodes with flavour
starts into this *avant-rap* about
metaphysical politics and *carnival-corn sweetness*
and I think *this clown's about thirty years ago*
but I might have one more spoonful
with cream
and do
and something happens
like a transplant (but not quite)
like an education (but more)
a newly opened window
dripping with spring dawn scent
and suddenly I see
(like I'm awake the whole time)
pictures sketched in charcoal
now vivid   animated
no longer inconspicuous
(you'd think having escaped
they would keep it quiet but
they were released   thrown out
to make as much noise
cause more of a disturbance
than any figment
any imagination
has ever caused)
so here they are
flaunting ripe clashes
coaxing attention from the sunshine
about to lose all hope of control

I look to the raspberry for guidance
but I've eaten it
and it's only the beginning

AN
ECHO
A
BOUT
TO
HAPPEN

she knew the meaning of meaning
& then forgot it
before she could tell it

I Wanted to be a Citizen of the World

Mostly
I've been talking
about the weather:

cold white liquid
and sad musical
a moan for barren trees
scratching the surface
of a pale afternoon

there should be
a death in the family.

October
is the slow death of seasons
vitality drains from rooftops
I grow scales
form opinions
do nothing to alter course

I no longer believe
in the weatherman

I've lost teeth
to the ice and
found illusion
under pillows

salt burns holes
in my tongue
I taste
          as I do.

A man sharpens edges
door to door

tell him how
in anger
I broke a window
bled on the floor
and changed nothing
but the temperature of the room.

He'll believe

it's a lie
though the bleeding
is real and internal
lung spleen kidney
melting

walk away

wonder
how cold
a man can be
without burial.

𝄽

Sometimes
I stand in line
all day
letting others
ahead.

𝄽

It's odd how
I never
remember names
someone told me
the trick is
to repeat

three times in the
immediate
conversation.

Strange –
how I never
remember names.

𝄽

I can cry at will

the idea bores me.

Late night
and I hear thunder
or the sound of moving furniture
the fine line between ceiling and floor

the people upstairs
are moving and
taking the hot water

the landlord is late
collecting rent
                again

to prove I live here
I barricade the door
and until you were so
unexpected that day and
out of the rain
no one knew

and even then
you were unsure
why I took so long

why the scraping
of wood on the floor and
I said *I'm not
proud of the room and
changed it for you*

you said nothing
only glanced at the desk
on its end
with a lamp

I said *a gift*
from a sculptor friend
a satire of the business world

you knew
I knew
you knew
I was lying.

I want to be
a citizen of the world
and the world
has no idea.

Predicted by a man
with sharp pencils and
satellite vision
I never occur.

In absence
I know nothing
but static and crossed lines:

Yes, I love you
but sometimes
I wish you would
please stop talking

convinced there is no such thing
as silence
and weighted by the thought
I fall
        sink to bottom
escaping restrictions
of weather and form
I grow to monstrous proportion
risk occasional appearance
and wait for the silence
of an echo about to happen

and then you
deeply beyond and swimming
against my understanding
of the current
of the tide
of October and the rain

and anyway
you are almost sure
there is no such thing as silence

Listen.
Cars drive by
on the wet street

Overcast

In this city
even through open windows
you can't hear the rain.
What I would do
for a little violence
in our weather.

Still
it's been like this all day —
unthundering

you come home to find me
staring through the drizzle
and with your hand
on my forehead
tell me
            I don't look well

how uplifting
and I can't say
how beautiful you are

only that the rain
is incomplete

Maps of the Migrating Hummingbird

I have forgotten the question:
something to do with
the ruin of beauty for science
the noble line of the monarch at rest

I am ten and the wind is steady
an easy reach in August
sitting on the foredeck
the dazzling light of a glass sun
and pointing home

a soft shock of colour
gusts low across the water
settles on the hatch beside me
its wings   folded and slightly frayed
withstand the wind that funnels through our sails
before lifting to fly a horizon
it cannot know will ever disappear

thirty   forty times this afternoon
I watch them one by one
cross the lake and on to Mexico
(though few return)
the water gaining depth with every path

(your friend thinks
hummingbirds migrate on the backs of Canada Geese
and is offended by my laughter
I want to believe her and more –
ninety beats per minute in formation
the hum and the honk)
harmony is silenced by solitary flight

in twenty years we haven't learned a thing
our sails butterfly the wind
and we drift a slow rocking wheel
the boom free and crashing with each jibe and tack
horizon lost in a haze of *was* and *will*
all distance being equal
we create our own whirlpool
I want this trip to never end

and you write from Costa Rica
sketches of a hummingbird kiss
mistaken for a flower and *buzzed*
your lines aspire to colour
letters land in the hallway
a folded whirlpool

Never Trust a Polar Bear in Shades

hoping a polar bear might take you for a seal
you buy a leather jacket for your trip north

I wear it this morning hunting milk for our coffee
the sun is up and your scent is strong
though my guide the store clerk
can't recall a recent sighting

the radio reports an Inuit elder couple
are charged by a polar bear and send it packing
their rifle jams so they wrestle
a straight-arm with a fist is a shield
bear won't bite your arm the long way
and the old man thinks he might have tickled it
a shock I suppose
                if you've never been tickled

the polar bear in the Calgary zoo is on prozac —
I wonder about Calgary
I might need it too –
I'm at the observation window
as the bear finds a pair of careless sunglasses
florescent green and plastic
tries to eat them or put them on
succeeding in the latter
on its back and *oh so cool*
when a woman —
concerned with fashion   digestion
or seeking the return of her property —
suggests the keeper enter the pit
and remove the offending spectacles
Lady a two ton bear wears what it wants

and I can see us wrestling bears some day
possibly on the same side
I'll concede *you're always right*
you'll admit *you don't know everything*
I won't ask you to shed your skin
and when I change the subject
                    you'll throw me a fish

Pas de Deux

how far we are waltzing south
the night plays bottleneck and spoon
or do we drift a northern river?

the invitation of water to draw
the notes of its passing
dripping your chin to my fingers

my skin in catching dissolves
pours into the shape you form
and understands new senses

or the fever that binds us
grandma's forgotten remedy unearthed
the reservoir purified

the herd saved
and the key to the city misplaced
assurance you say *is the line of our shoulders*

and cured we're wound within
you borrow my lungs for a moment
I swallow your purr

the way you finish my sentences
free from whole truth
you allow discovery

As you are only four hundred years old

you won't remember this first lagoon
the heat dripping ferns
or the song playing on the radio
as we wash into the still wet air

and maybe it's why you choose mystery for pleasure

centuries precipitate on your lower lip
a catalyst to your lungs' excavation:

    the sand castle we find buried in the surf
    and the people who live there
    themselves unable to resist
    peering through tiny keyholes
    trying to remember their own soft mornings
    and that first   lingering taste

And we'll all go together
To pull wild mountain thyme
All around the purple heather
Will ye go lassie go

Before we are known to write letters

when light is the dusk of sandstone
and quiet a dance to the hidden voice of mountains

the cool tongue of April calls

Oh the summer time is coming
And the leaves are sweetly turning
And the wild mountain thyme
Blooms around the purple heather
Will ye go lassie go

didn't know you could fly did you
dissolve over emerald lakes
land   fingers through moss and loose earth

take my hand
I'll race you to the edge   and lose
(only by a step)
and falling will never be so sudden fear
ice   and clear
your diamond tremble

I will build my love a bower
By yon clear and crystal fountain
And on it I will shower
All the flowers of the mountain
Will ye go lassie go

will tenderness let slip a lace secret of underbrush dew
coyote fade from the shadows of late campfire folk songs
look now
dawn comes a blend of last ember
the clear run of peak to stream
the trailing voice of an old story teller's love song

> *Will ye go lassie go*
> *And we'll all go together*
> *To pull wild mountain thyme*
> *All around the purple heather*
> *Will ye go lassie go*

A Gift

How far will we see the eclipse by now
(the evening's edge while buffed with frost)
and curling in our over-stuffed
drinking something hot and thick

a recipe of my concoction

(and after all I ever wanted)
to find behind your ear
the music a breath might make
if breath is a second wet snow

a thumb tip silver tinder box
open it
                free the light of animated moon
(over so many years)
I never should have promised
what I hope for

softly
may I return the senses
to chocolate and smooth skin

may I untie
(simple as the ribbon you wear)
how you send me
                        open
                                to begin

THE HI STORY OF E LEC TRIC LIGHT

whenever I draw a circle
I immediately want
to step out of it

The Gospel According to Jonathan Smith
(no relation)

Only a factory town
the sun doesn't set
it loses itself in shadows
the moon crouched in doorways
waits to eliminate the competition

the end of any back street
finds grey stacked on grey
framing the final installment
in the history of electric light.

Inside:
television
knickknacks
a set table
knives forks spoons
silver sometimes
(in a drawer with a key turned once a year)
paper napkins
a dish rack
maybe enough hot water.

A shift.

Headlights follow faded-blue silhouettes
from a smokestack centerpiece
cinders ribbon the sky
form a black path through the night
and carry on
until everything is deserted streets.

Outside the factory
someone murders a trash can
for spilling its guts.

voices leak over the sidewalk
seep into cracks
and grow like weeds

listen

someone is downstairs reading
the ride of Paul Revere

a busy signal
a phone off the hook.

wives and husbands wait
for husbands and wives

lovers set roses on fire
pick and burn
reach to a future where
answers are there for the asking
and not there

a siren
another siren
a faded blue accident

a crime
a trash can kicked down
a siren.

And someone downstairs reading
the ride of Paul Revere

and somewhere downstairs
mushroom cloud
the pride of all our fear
and someone upstairs making noise
no carpet under bedposts –
try the floor (but it creaks too) –
a sound released of sweat and love
a sound not quite remembered

follow it
corner it
bottle it
it can be sold
for nickels and dimes
to children
who twist at the neck
and rub into open pores
who listen
who listen to all those others
some of them teachers
who listen to someone downstairs
reading passages from
the midnight ride of Paul Revere

wide-eyed open remember
believing what's put in front of you
or you'll have it for breakfast.

Dad was never one for Sesame Street
too many shades on the black and white
Mom said he was colour-blind
but I know why he never read me stories.

Another shift.

Someone reads the instructions on a punch clock
get it right the first time
the hands move ahead without telling and
now he reads the minutes' tick
by twenty years of coffee on the quarter hour and
thirty years of lunch noon to twelve-thirty and
forty years of whistle blows
time to go

I'm expected for dinner
though there's time for *maybe one*
quickly inside
the peeling back entrance
Ladies With Escorts Only
to a lounge life
where firestrip ciders
attend worn opinion
where a cockroach
knows the argument and adapts
it's his job
and he doesn't make change

where *last call* is
the silence of empty tables

Turn out the lights
Lock the door

Landmarks

at some point
we all turn wrong at a gas station
two lights   a left at the yellow barn
understand what colour is to direction
the red lines we draw on maps

and watching a rerun of last year's World Series
the slow motion replay as Carter rounds third
do you notice the fan on the field?
he'll always be able to stop the tape and say
That's me   tackled in the foreground
I was charged and fined
now I have answers for everything.

The first time the Jays won the Series
I was at Mac's schoolhouse near Wellington
and found my cat Crazy in a tree.
From there it follows:
the location of my first kick
blues radio when Lennon died

if we remember achievement
what if I say *Oswald   Chapman*
the Jays lose that Series

what happens later when I say
he wasn't that great a president
there are bigger tragedies
get over it

There is a deep blue boulevard

where no stars hang
and the atmosphere drips
too cold to call rain

where sidewalks barely
remember where they've been
shifting slow and cracked
as if attempting cobblestone

windows wide and wider
overflow with
no one ever wanted
enough room for reflection

diners serve applehood
and mother pie
twenty-four
                    seven

curtains
            wings closed on landing
                    a single flight
absorb light
and the meaning of inside jokes.

There is a dark dream boulevard
where children wait
solitude hanging from their shirt sleeves
as if they stopped playing for a moment
a million years ago
heard their names called
from the wonder of curtains
and held their breath
turning a deep shade of blue

The Women Outside Bruno's School of Hair Design
... I Wonder

to hold an empty coffee cup for warmth
look in the grounds
and tell the future

the broken heel in your handbag

I remember the heat
your walk-up over Anna's Academy of Dance
the open window to the place next door
and the neighbours we never saw
who new us   I think
sweat soaked
there was nothing else we could do those nights
and I loved them

there is a cockroach in my pocket
the night you limped
a broken heel and falling
a roach I blamed and killed
I keep it with me

I never saw anyone take lessons
no step charts on the floor
and all these years   still here
has to be a front for something
you never made a safe decision
and you paid

your first drink in six years
your number isn't listed
you wouldn't give the name of the motel

the old Hungarian must have made this corner
with leather hands
his Harbord Shoe repair
the bank machine that replaced it
this cockroach   those lab coats

and no one's learning how to dance

look
       through your heat-stroked hair

tell me the future

Bicarbonate Of Sex

The barnacle's a hermaphrodite
(I'm not making accusations)
hitched for life to rock or rust
it filter feeds

and after a period of time
if male enough
it extends an organ five times the length of its shell
and visits immediate neighbours
until it finds one feeling particularly female

foolish to suggest a mollusc feels anything
this comes from a documentary on TV
and the narrator is excited
without providing detailed explanation

so while you imagine
a thirty foot penis groping around the room
trying to determine who swings which way
I'll worry what we'd do if we couldn't dance.

Are your eyes natural?

You are the most fluid eyes I have ever seen.
You are the ocean in the Virgins.
I sail catamarans.
                    (clear)

You cause a constellation above my bed
everyone falls for the *same old line*
I think you are crazy
if I know you aren't true
and my hair is natural.

Someone tells a friend
in Cleveland   men buy women drinks
to which he replies
in Toronto men buy women bowling shoes

and if there's no bowling
where do we first date?
hitched to a rock and flailing legs

there's a little blue pill for impotent men
and in France   an orgasm pill for women
one day we drop them in the same glass of water
and stir
          problems arise
the male dissolves before the female hits bottom
the glass leaks and we hardly know each other

good thing I believe everything you say
as you roll your eyes past stars
where I have never been

The night Cosby goes off air

I set the house on fire

unintentional act:
thinking the TV in sight
I pull a pistol
empty six chambers
and miss every god-damned time
ricochet sparks recycle
stacks of aging newspaper
the heat is rampant

Jenny glares at me
loses patience
and leaves the room

sitting for a moment
I muse on bucket brigades
and look for Jenny's return
with a hose under pressure
a shining red hat

smoke dances itself up curtains

I struggle from my chair
and scour shelves
to remember anything worth saving
not a book or shirt
a few singed letters
my records melt
forty-five thirty-three seventy-eight

the plastic air of lamp shades
and paper walls
follows from room to room

holding my breath
I run through hallways and stairwells
passing Jenny as she
tears support from the bannister
she seems to shimmer
in the erratic light
a gas flame flicker
about to go out

the roof caves in between us

I scatter
break windows
kick doors
choke outside
the sound of raging timber
and Jenny
            stirring there
selling axe handles
to the firemen

Suite: Mustard

Good Friday the thirteenth
cool for spring
partly cloudy
I will not visit the sick

hospitals are ammonia
I have a bottle of chlorine bleach
a gas mask
and an interest
in lingering habits

senseless violence
and the long weekend

My friend Mike caused a war
by dropping a quarter
pulling a handle
and pressing an off-hand bet

the jackpot came up tombstones
(that's when the shooting started)

it wasn't what he had in mind
he's against war generally
but it happens so quickly
and now
            there is mud

the pale mustard
of abandoned construction sights
sitting targets
knee deep
sink over time
until in relief —
head slightly back and to the left —
stretched arms curl across the surface
as if around friends so important
they've never been told

and now he's taken the blame
my friend Mike seems shorter
his shoulders bow the catapult's ballistic curve

he washes his hands a lot
he smokes cigarettes
he won't reach in the dark

Sorry
      I forgot your drink
a waitress
her spill cloth circling
wiping my reflection from the table

After the last (stupid) war
(is over)
everyone says
Merry Christmas
or something
very much like that
and then goes back
to work on Monday

I watch old gangster films
each time
disappointed

never sure of the good guys

after all
no one really wins the lottery

it's more
the struggle to buy a ticket

The geese are back early this year
he said
then raised his twelve-gauge
shot down spring

Ahimsa

Pour clean the Ganges
milk   flour   Gandhi's ash
inter custom
            the yield of banks.

Asked his impression of western civilization
he thought
            it would be a good idea

and that was when?
the thirties?
where are we in our fast?

our golden trees are fallen
our bronze swing sounding by the quart
the splinter of ballots burning

**Leaves are done the bonfire
on Daniel Hatchet's grave**

died eighteen fifty-seven
he's cremated every autumn
ashes are just memories
for the wind.

Black cat on the porch step
the house next door's for sale

a chance of coffins in the basement
trap door to the attic
and they'll take any offer
they just can't stand the smoke.

The price ghosts demand for haunting
the cornfield's skeleton corps
is waiting orders
to be buried where it stands.

Dogs dig rodents.

And sunset's grey green marble
closes black the inside of a body bag
sound suffocates with slow muffled spasms
the musk of bogs and railway tracks
the chill air twig snap
of old bones shifting weight

and Hatchet's tombstone
aging with soot

why
the
stegosaur
us
is my
favourite
dinosaur

A small boy walks backwards in the rain
humming a music
   distant from notes I might string together
late for school
oblivious to everything
but the pauses in his song.

Yesterday
leaves slipped on the wind
matted they cling to the red-brick heels
of black rubber boots
and hold on desperately
for any hope a boy can give

with careful steps
he turns
avoids cracks worms and weeds
until the plastic of his hat is lifted in the air
spinning him again

on the uneven sidewalk
he scrapes summer from his sole.

He believes in dinosaurs
not only that they once roamed freely
(as cats between fenceposts)
but that they still live
                         fiercely
in schoolyards
and sleep
he's seen the footprints
and will show you
if you let him

great herds of terrible horns and teeth
breaking trails to the wonder of
where they are in the day

Extinct
his father says.

Imagine Stegosaurus:

a walnut brain
steering the bulk of an elephant

ancient and awkward herds
circling to protect the young

not an exact science

a herbivore
a relative of birds

the power and balance
of a long spiked tail

intrigue
a protruding plate
solar attraction to the cold-blooded morning

the ugly likeliness
                    of its expression.

Consider a conversation with myself
mumbling on about the mesozoic
the rise of flowering plants
the death of the dinosaur.
Balance your diet.
Eat a vegetarian.
Sixty-five million years
the only wisdom for carnivores
and not an acceptable answer.

Someone says
Not this Monday
but Monday next...
and I wait
through an ice-age
and a drought

and no one says
The dinosaur
lovely as the world's first flower
and I am aware of more than emptiness
or the want of fallen lovers.

I see the sound of the pause
in a child's hummed notes
the invisible
beginning in the lungs
and fading with the sunset

bewildered under stars
I blunder backwards through millennia
and know only the magic
of believing the impossible.

The rain stops
            for the last time maybe
the wind
singing a wrong and difficult key
leaves museum skeletons
bleached and marrowless branches
peeled bark
the discovery of fire

the wind
a spiral in the corner of a schoolyard
a challenge to the freedom of leaves

why is the Stegosaurus my favourite dinosaur?

watching a small boy
late   in no hurry
I'm lost in a lifetime of ages
and I know
it has something to do
with the danger
of the tail

Liner Notes

♪ indicates tracks available in Stereo on *The Sound of Filling Hollow*

THE EPIGRAMS

   p 5: as told by Art Blakey
   pp 22 & 58: R. Buckminster 'Bucky' Fuller
   p 40: Carl Sandburg

THE CHARTS

   'Blue Boulevard' & 'Talkin' bout the Weather'
   by Tim Posgate

All events depicted are true.

Acknowledgements

The author was supported in the writing of these poems by the Canada Council for the Arts Writers' Development program, by the Ontario Arts Council Work In Progress and Writers' Reserve programs and by the recommendations of the Dave & Sue Allen Foundation.

Thanks to everyone who helped administer the above. Thanks also to my Writers' Reserve recommenders: *Books In Canada*, Brick Books, *Descant*, *The New Quarterly*, Penumbra Press, and Wolsak & Wynn.

Most of the poems were first read aloud at the following venues: Apostles' Bar, Banff Centre, Blancmange, Bohemian Embassy III, Café May, Commercial Street Arts Festival (Vancouver), Hillside Music Festival (Guelph), Idler Pub, Princess Theatre (Waterloo), Port Townsend Writers' Festival (Washington St), Rivoli & at Scream In High Park.

Some of the poems have appeared at various stages of evolution in the following publications: *The Apostle's Bar*, Imprint, *The Last Word*, *A Letter To His Excellency Nicky Drumbolis*, *The New Quarterly*, *Oversion*, *Quarry*, *Queen Street Quarterly*, *sinovertan*, *This* Magazine, *Tidepool*.

'The Women Outside Bruno's ...' appeared out of The Mermaid Tavern as a clandestine chapbook. 'Why The Stegosaurus ...' appears on *RE/New: a CD-ROM Journal of Poetry*, and was used as a TV Ontario artistic vignette; a poorly edited version appeared in *Carnival: a Scream In High Park Reader*. 'Pas de Deux' was commissioned for the CD / booklet / performance *An Eager Leap* by guitarist Tim Posgate. 'Ahimsa' is Sanskrit and is the ethical principle of noninjury to both people and animals.

Thanks

At some point in my life, somewhere between high-school sports and the math degree, I decided the only important contribution I could make to this bobbing little planet is to, one day, write a good poem. A goal that naturally requires unending support in all manners from everyone and everything around me. Arrogant? Certainly. Self-centred and probably obnoxious on occasion (hey, I was young). And yet, it is my fortune to be surrounded by open, giving, honest people who believe I might actually pull it off. Thank you. I hope some day to justify your faith.

To those who have helped me ramble through life: Mom & Dad who hold faith despite more evidence to the contrary than anyone else, the grey squirrel, my brother Patrick who keeps me in bass line, write fiction, my sister Andrea, the shadows are crazy at midnight, Gayle Irwin, the hum-soft morning, the sum of the parts, Helen Tsiriotakis, Dave & Sue Allen, *living large in a small world*, Kemal & Bernadette Al-jbouri, Dave & Theresa Holden, Schtick & Denise, Pete Sero, *19/04/64*, Mark & Sharon Higgins, Cas Flis, Harold Bulmanis, Debbie Lillico, Leslie Webster, Captain Video & the Cathode Ray Boys, take it all as a joke and figure it out later, Ivan 'jive' Beekmans, Steve & Phil (*SF, NY* ...), numbers, tone man, Suzanne Carrell, Barb Dametto, Jody Baltessen, Sherry Hergott, Dave & Scotty & Blis & the boys on the soccer team, Fabian Kean, The McPhees, The Banks, The Brants & The Yewchucks & Sunday afternoon ball hockey.

To those who contribute to the art and ensure there is an audience: Bill Kennedy, Seán Virgo, John Barlow, Stan Rogal, Death Waits, David Warren, Jacob Wren, Mac McArthur, Steve Heighton, Paul Dutton, Susan Helwig, Wayne Ray, Allan Briesmaster, Barb Baldwin, Richard Kenney, the sweatshop crowd, Nancy Bullis, Michael Tweed, Luciano Iocabelli, the Café May crowd, Stephen Pender (:), Nancy Dembowski, Clive Thompson, Darren Wershler-Henry, Alexandra Leggat, Matthew Remski, Michael Holmes, everyone involved with Scream In High Park, Eddy Yanofsky, Tom MacKay, Alana Wilcox, Richard Vaughan, Lorraine Filyer, Steve Venright, Stuart Ross, Judy MacDonald, Mike O'Connor, Jennie Punter, Stephen Cain, Suzanne Zelazo, Nicky Drumbolis, Beth & Joy Learn, Richard Preston, Henry Martinuk, his uneven rhythm, sara craig, Selina Martin, Tim Posgate, Kenny Kirkwood, Saulius Fidleris, Liz Hart, Brent Bodrug, Tricia Postle, Adam Nashman, Chris Wodskou, Coach House, especially Stan Bevington & Victor Coleman who asked for this book as it would become.

In memory of the late Shaunt Basmajian (& jwc for 'Shaunt's Hat'). There are lines in here for all of you. May they find you well.

Typeset in Bodoni Six and Letter Gothic and printed at Coach House on bpNichol Lane.

Editor for the Press: Victor Coleman

Designed by Darren Wershler-Henry and Bill Kennedy

Cover art by Beth Learn

Author photo and cover of *The Sound of Filling Hollow* by Gayle Irwin

To read the online version of this text and other titles from Coach House Books, visit our website:

www.chbooks.com

To add your name to our e-mailing list, write:

mail@chbooks.com

Toll-free: 1 800 367 6360

Conventional mail:

Coach House Books
401 Huron (rear) on bpNichol Lane
Toronto, Ontario
M5S 2G5